A Victorian Sampler
Of Works By
Diana Bold

This is a work of fiction. Names, characters, places, and incidents are products of the author's imagination or are used fictitiously and are not to be construed as real. Any resemblance to actual events, locales, organizations, or persons, living or dead, is entirely coincidental.

Masked Intentions

By Diana Bold

Gambling on the Duke's Daughter

By Diana Bold

Copyright July 2022

Cover Artist: Sadie Bosque

Author's Note

I hope you enjoy these samples of MASKED INTENTIONS, the first book in my UNMASKING PROMETHEUS series, and GAMBLING ON THE DUKE'S DAUGHTER, the first book in my BRIDES OF SCANDAL series. You can find the full version of both books for free on all major eBook retailers, and both are also available in print.

Happy reading!
Diana Bold

MASKED INTENTIONS
Prologue

December 1879

Adrian Strathmore sat upon the hard stone floor, his knees drawn to his thin chest. Lightning flashed through the tower windows of the oldest part of the Earl of Winters's ancient manor house, illuminating the pale, terrified faces of his two brothers. He hated that they were there.

Their mother had remarried nearly two years ago, but Morgan and Lucien had been away at school except for the holidays. Tonight was the first time their stepfather, Nigel Croft, the Earl of Winters, had tried to hurt Adrian when they'd been home. Lucien, who was only fifteen, but had become the Earl of Hawkesmere after their real father's death, had tried to protect Adrian, only to be brutally debased and humiliated himself instead. Adrian wanted to hide himself away somewhere and weep with shame.

"Are you all right, Luke?" Thirteen-year-old Morgan, Adrian's twin, broke the silence, his voice tentative. "Do you need a doctor?"

Lucien shook his head, obviously horrified at the thought of anyone else, even a doctor, knowing what his stepfather had done to him. "I'm fine," he muttered. "In a few days... I'm sure I'll be fine."

"We should tell Mother," Morgan persisted. "She won't let this happen again. She'll take us back to Hawkesmere. She'll never let that bastard touch you again."

"She can't leave," Lucien said. "He's her husband. And she'd never believe us anyway. She's in love with him."

Adrian remained silent, shrinking farther into himself with each word Lucien said. He'd been badly burned in the fire that had taken their father's life three years ago. Terrible scars covered the left side of his face, as well as his chest and left shoulder. For many months after the accident, he'd clung to the precipice between life and death. The experience had changed him. He'd become a creature of shadows, observing but never participating. He hadn't spoken a single word since his father's death.

When the twins had turned twelve and were old enough to go to boarding school with Lucien at Abingdon, Winters had gently reminded their mother that the school was reserved for Britain's best and brightest. He'd assured her that Adrian, with his burns and silence, wouldn't fit in. Their mother had agreed, and Adrian had been forced to remain in the nursery, with baby Allison, which was humiliating for a boy his age.

Adrian's silence had triggered their stepfather's latest attack. Earl Winters made no secret of his hatred for his stepchildren, except when their mother was around, but he saved most of his anger for Adrian. Tonight he'd dragged all three boys, and his own son, seventeen-year-old Roger, to this tower in the oldest wing of his ancient house, where no one could hear their cries. Then he and Roger had set about breaking Adrian—demanding that he speak, calling him horrible names. When their nasty insults had failed to elicit a response, the earl had proceeded to beat him, as he so often did, while Roger looked on with barely disguised glee. Unable to bear it, Lucien had gathered his courage and dared to step between them, only to have the earl turn that fury against him.

"How can she love him?" Morgan asked, his voice laced with bitterness. "He's nothing like Father."

Adrian didn't want to think about their father. Even after all this time, the pain of losing him was fresh. And he didn't see the need to point out the obvious. Their mother was a weak-willed, foolish woman who needed a man—any man—to be happy.

"Adrian," Lucien whispered, his voice raw with suspicion. "What happened to me tonight—does he do that to you all the time?"

Adrian squeezed his eyes tightly shut, then nodded and buried his ruined face in the crook of his arm. His slim body shook, buffeted by an icy wind drifting in through one of the windows. Another round of thunder split the air around them as the storm continued to rage outside.

Morgan made a wordless sound of denial and moved to Adrian's side, wrapping him in a fierce embrace, murmuring to him in the strange, made-up language the two of them had spoken as toddlers. This comfort, after so many months of loneliness and despair, finally spurred Adrian to speak. He had to tell them. He couldn't keep it all locked inside any longer.

"There's a Greek story I read once..."

At the sound of Adrian's rough, stuttering voice, Morgan pulled away. He and Lucien stared at their usually silent brother as though they'd seen a ghost.

"About Prometheus," Adrian continued. "Do you know it?"

After a long moment of stunned surprise, Lucien gave a jerky nod. "Isn't he the fellow who stole the fire from the gods?"

Adrian lifted his head and wiped the tears from his cheeks with a shaking hand. "I was thinking more about how he was chained to a rock and got his liver eaten out every day by an eagle."

"Is that what it's been like?" Morgan put his arm around Adrian's thin shoulders again, his face filled with anguish. "Why didn't you tell us?"

"What good would that have done?" Adrian shrugged away, embarrassed and ashamed. "He's just going to keep hurting us. There's nothing we can do."

"Alone, none of us can do anything," Lucien said slowly. "But there are three of us. Together, we could do anything."

The twins listened attentively as Lucien outlined a plan that would free them from their stepfather's tyranny, yet allow them to remain anonymous if things should go wrong. Together they would create a masked crusader, a powerful facade they could don at will.

Quiet intensity vibrated in Adrian's voice as he volunteered to contribute his rather stunning scientific knowledge to the endeavor. He spoke of designing weapons and other amazing gadgetry. The prospect of slaying his dragon had brought about a transformation. Gone was the frightened, silent little boy. His voice grew stronger with every word he spoke.

Not to be outdone, Morgan found a piece of charcoal in the fireplace and sketched a remarkably detailed image of a masked man upon the crumbling wall.

"What shall we call ourselves?" Lucien asked, the horror of the evening dissipating in the rush of excitement their planning had caused.

Morgan and Adrian shared a look and came to complete agreement.

"Prometheus," Adrian answered.

And so Prometheus was born...

Chapter One

March 1896

For the third time in as many weeks, Adrian Strathmore sat in the shadowy corner of his family's private box at the St. James's Theatre on Duke Street, gazing at the dazzling, raven-haired actress who took her bow on the stage below.

Miss Vanessa Bourke had taken London by storm during the past few months, but Adrian doubted anyone had become quite as captivated by her as he. Since the first time he'd seen her play Celia in *As You Like It*, she'd become the object of both his admiration and desire. She acted the part with a noble purity of spirit that called to something deep inside him. She haunted his dreams and provided a brief respite from the carefully laid plans of destruction that filled his days.

Not that a woman like her could ever be his, of course. Even his family's wealth and power were not enough to camouflage his many flaws, both the obvious physical scars and the ones deep inside him. Eyes tracked him in the dark, those who were far more interested in catching a glimpse of the Earl of Hawkesmere's disfigured little brother than watching the play. He sank deeper into his seat, despising their curiosity, wishing for anonymity. All he'd ever truly wanted was to be able to walk through a crowd without anyone staring.

In stark comparison, the rushlights lit Miss Bourke's face with an ethereal glow, and her dark, gypsy eyes flashed with pleasure as another round of applause shook the building. She lived for this moment, relished the adoration of the crowd.

Overwhelmed by loneliness, he brought a single yellow rose to his lips and then tossed it far below him, upon the stage at Miss Bourke's feet.

* * * *

Vanessa Bourke reached down and picked up the yellow rose, blinking against the glare of the rushlights as she searched the private box to stage right. There. In the corner. A flicker of movement. But no matter how hard she tried, she couldn't see her latest admirer's face. The box belonged to the Earl of Hawkesmere, but the theater gossips said the man who occupied it tonight was the earl's younger brother, a man who'd been scarred by a fire when he was a child.

As the curtain came down, Marcus Colby, the leading man, gave her a sardonic smile. "Another rose, darling? It appears your beauty has snared the beast."

"Jealousy doesn't become you," she retorted, hurrying toward her dressing room to remove her greasy makeup. Exhaustion pulled at her like a heavy weight, and she wanted nothing more than to return to her tiny flat just a few blocks away and tumble into bed.

"He seems quite taken with you," Marcus continued, trailing behind her with languid grace. "They say he's rich as Croesus but quite mad."

Vanessa pulled open her dressing room door and gestured to the dozens of flower arrangements filling every available surface. "He's hardly the only one to give me flowers."

Marcus gave the display a dismissive glance. "He's the only aristocrat."

Vanessa glared at her friend. In a moment of wine and weakness, she'd told him of her goal to find a rich husband. He'd been playing matchmaker ever since.

"He's hardly in a position to be particular," Marcus continued, lowering his voice. "With his money, you could have the security you want. You could leave all this and start a family, though it still makes no sense to me why you'd want to shackle yourself down that way."

The mention of a family sent the usual pang of longing skittering through her veins. She'd grown up in abject poverty, and when her mother had died, she'd been sent to live with her father, a drunken struggling actor she'd never met. She'd spent the rest of her childhood dragged from theater to theater, constantly moving, going from feast to famine and back again. Much as she loved the stage, she'd long dreamt of a stable life, one that didn't depend on the fickle love of the crowd. She was nearly twenty-five. Soon her beauty would fade, and she'd have a hard time finding roles. If she didn't find a man she could raise a family with before that happened, she feared she never would.

She strode to the mirror and began the arduous process of removing the makeup, hoping Marcus would take the hint and go away. Instead, his elegant hand curled around her shoulder, squeezing lightly. "I just hate to see you so depressed, darling."

"I know." She shut her eyes against a sudden rush of tears. "I appreciate it, Marc. I really do. But no knight in shining armor is going to save me. I have to save myself."

He brushed a swift kiss to her temple. "Get some sleep. It's a good thing the theater's dark tomorrow. You're looking a bit peaked." When she glared at him again, he laughed and threw his hands up in surrender. "Good night, 'Nessa."

"Good night." She gave him a grudging smile. For all his teasing, she knew he had her best interests at heart. As soon as he left the room, she picked up the yellow rose she'd tossed aside and placed it carefully in a cut-glass vase with two others from her mysterious admirer.

* * * *

Adrian leaped from the roof of Hawley's Gentlemen's Club, wincing as a hail of gunfire erupted from the street below. He landed hard on a sloping overhang of the building next door, scrambling to gain his footing without dropping the small boy in his arms. He pressed his palm to the sharp prick of pain in his left thigh and felt the wetness of his own blood.

The bastards had shot him!

Flames swept across the club's facade, temporarily distracting the men who'd given chase. Adrian gazed at the brilliant, dangerous light, both fascinated and terrified, as always. His brothers did not understand his penchant for using fire to destroy these hellholes, but how could they? He didn't understand it himself.

Satisfaction burned bright within him as he viewed the destruction he'd wrought. Since he'd set the fire in the attic, everyone had been able to get out safely, but for a few nights, at least, the scum who frequented the club would not be able to slake their lust on children.

Tightening his hold on the boy he'd rescued from that prison, he concentrated on his escape, more than a bit disturbed by the fact that his prey seemed to have been ready for him this time. He'd have to figure out how later. For now, the only thing that mattered was getting the boy to safety.

The child remained eerily quiet as Adrian leaped from roof to roof. Despite Adrian's assurances, he doubted the boy realized he'd been rescued, enduring the situation with a blank-eyed acceptance that broke what remained of Adrian's heart.

Adrian had managed to put no more than half a dozen blocks between himself and the club when the sounds of pursuit intensified. He paused for a moment in the shadow of a chimney, breathing heavily with pain and exhaustion as he weighed his options.

His leg ached unbearably, and dizziness threatened to overwhelm him. God knew how much blood he'd lost. He needed a place to lie low until his pursuers lost interest. As he took stock of his surroundings, a ludicrous idea took root in his mind.

Vanessa Bourke lived a few streets over, in a once-opulent mansion that had seen its better days and had been split into half a dozen flats. He'd made it his business to know, even though he'd assumed the information would prove useless.

What would she do if he were to show up uninvited, dressed as Prometheus? Would she turn him away, or would she take him in and bandage his wound? Could he use the child to gain her trust? He would never make it to Brookhaven Orphanage in his current condition.

Telling himself he had no other choice, he headed toward Miss Bourke's flat.

* * * *

A clamor at the window woke Vanessa from a deep sleep. She sat straight up in bed, heart hammering in her chest as she peered through the darkness toward the source of the sound. She'd left her window cracked in an attempt to catch a cooling breeze, but now it was fully open, the curtains fluttering in the wind.

At the foot of her bed, she sensed a presence, a dark shape melding with the shadows. "Is someone there?" Her voice trembled with fear, and she edged toward her nightstand, where she kept a small, loaded pistol.

The shadow moved, stepping forward into a faint patch of moonlight. "Shhh," a deep male voice whispered. "I won't hurt you."

A sudden commotion sounded in the alley beneath the window as a group of men thundered through the usually quiet neighborhood. Dogs howled as sharp voices barked orders down below.

They're looking for this man, who has taken refuge in my room.

A new rush of fear washed through her. What sort of criminal was he? And more importantly, what did he want with her?

Tension spiraled between them as the shouts continued, then slowly faded off into the distance.

After what seemed an eternity, the stranger gave a weary-sounding sigh and then abruptly struck a match, casting a small puddle of light as he looked around. "Thank you," he murmured, as he flicked on the gas lights and put out the match. "If you would have screamed, they'd have caught us."

Us? She gave another nervous glance around the room, but he appeared to be alone. He turned toward her, and she got her first glimpse of the intruder. She drew in a sharp breath because his features were hidden by a fanciful mask of sparkling ivory and bone. The tall, broad-shouldered man wore a crimson cape, the deep color of blood.

Prometheus. She recognized the fearsome bandit from the newspaper sketches. He'd burned down dozens of brothels and rescued children who'd been pressed to work in them against their will. Though the police wanted nothing more than to capture him, he'd become a hero to the people.

She crossed her arms over her chest, very aware of her state of undress. "They're gone now."

"I'll leave as soon as it's safe," he assured her. "In the meantime, do you mind if I lay the child down?" He swept back his cloak, revealing a young boy asleep in his arms.

The child was as beautiful as an angel, with dark, curly hair. He couldn't have been more than six or seven. Her stomach turned at the thought of what had been done to the poor boy. Giving a jerky nod, she scooted over to make room. "Put him here," she whispered.

Prometheus tenderly lowered the child to the bed, then returned his attention to Vanessa. "Do you have anything I can use for a bandage?"

"A bandage?" Some of her fear evaporated when he gestured to his left thigh and parted his crimson cape to reveal that the dark trousers beneath were soaked through with blood. "My God, have you been shot?"

He nodded briefly and sank into a chair. She scrambled off the far side of the bed, reaching for the heavy satin robe that lay draped across her footboard. Wrapping it tightly around her, she bit her lip. "May I get some things to tend to you?"

He nodded again, and she hurried down the hall. The thought of escape only crossed her mind briefly as she wet a washcloth and split an old white sheet to use as a bandage. She didn't think he'd hurt her, and there was the child to consider.

"I'll help you with your wound," she told him when she returned. "But then you really must go."

"Thank you, Miss Bourke," he said softly.

"You know my name?" Her fears returned full force. Had he picked her flat on purpose?

He bowed his head, ripping his trouser leg to reveal a deep bloody hole. "I recognize you," he murmured. "I've seen you play Celia half a dozen times."

Heat rushed to her cheeks, along with a strange sort of pleasure. This man, who was making a difference, who put his life on the line for those less fortunate, had recently sat in the dark and watched her perform.

She crossed nervously to his side and handed him the wet cloth, along with the strips of sheet he could use as a bandage.

"You should have that looked at as soon as possible. You mustn't let it get infected."

He took the wet cloth and swabbed at the blood, hissing a bit with the pain the pressure must have caused. "The bullet passed through. I'll be all right. I just need to get home where I can clean it properly."

She stared at the lower half of his face, the chiseled lips and strong chin revealed beneath the demi-mask. She'd lay odds he was devastatingly handsome.

When he made another soft sound of pain, she knelt beside him and took the cloth from his blood-streaked hands. "Here. Let me do it."

He sank back against the chair, closing his eyes. "I hoped you'd be this way," he whispered. "When I got hurt, I thought if I could just get here, to you, you would help me."

She wanted to ask him why he'd thought that and how he'd known where to find her but thought those questions better left unanswered. "I've read about you in the papers," she said instead. "I think what you're doing is very brave and needs to be done."

His lips quirked in a brief smile. "Well, I wish my friends at Scotland Yard felt the same. Between them and the bastards who work at the brothel, I felt as though I was running for my life tonight."

She bound his leg with the length of bandage, using a piece of red ribbon to bind it firmly in place. "There. That should hold until you get home." She glanced up and found him watching her, his face mere inches from her own.

"Thank you," he told her, his gaze intent behind the mask. She couldn't tell what color his eyes were, but she thought they must be blue or green because they caught the light. "There's something else you can do for me if you would."

"Depends on what it is," she answered cautiously, knowing she'd probably helped him far too much already.

"It will be all I can do to make it home tonight." The deep, masculine rumble of his voice sent shivers down her spine. "If I take the child to Brookhaven, I fear I'll either collapse or be caught. Do you think you could take him there in the morning? It's the orphanage on Field Street in Kensington. Just tell them Prometheus sent you. They won't ask any questions."

She bit her lip doubtfully. There seemed to be no harm in what he was asking. The theater was dark tomorrow, so she had the day free. She could hire a hack to deliver the boy—a small price to pay to keep him safe from the lechers who'd had him before. Besides, she would hate to think of Prometheus getting caught.

"Yes," she agreed, surprised by her own daring. "I'll do it."

He reached out and brushed his fingertips across her jaw. "Miss Bourke, you've been an angel."

She caught her breath, trying to see behind the mask to discern the color of his eyes more clearly. Her heart pounded furiously in her chest.

Then he bent forward and kissed her. At first, his lips pressed sweetly, chastely against hers, giving her plenty of time to pull away. When she foolishly did not, he leaned closer, wrapping one arm around her shoulders and pulling her against him, deepening the kiss with a groan.

Nothing this exciting had ever happened to her. Kissing a masked stranger in her room in the middle of the night seemed surreal, impossible to believe.

After a few blissful minutes, he pulled away. She lifted one hand to her lips, stunned. She'd never felt such an overwhelming attraction to a man, yet she hadn't even seen his face.

"So sweet," he said, his voice a bit unsteady. "I'll never forget you, Miss Bourke."

Before she could respond, he turned and left her flat the way he'd come, through the window.

Chapter Two

Adrian sank gingerly into a chair in front of the roaring fire in his bedchamber, exhausted and in more pain then he wanted to admit. The trip home from Miss Bourke's flat had sapped the last of his strength. He lifted his hips and stripped off his tattered trousers, frowning when he saw how much blood had soaked through the bandage. If he were wise, he would send for a doctor, but he didn't know of anyone he could trust as much as Clinton, his longtime butler.

In a few moments, he'd ring for Clinton to help him clean and stitch the wound, but for now, he just wanted a few quiet moments to relive the brief time he'd spent with Miss Bourke. Running a finger along the satin ribbon she'd used on the bandage, he thought of the way she'd melted into his kiss, the soft, breathy sound she'd made as he'd pulled her into his arms. For the first time in his adult life, his scars hadn't mattered. The mask had given him the anonymity he craved.

Of course, she never would have given herself so sweetly if she knew the truth, if she knew Prometheus was Adrian Strathmore. But perhaps, if he could arrange a few more meetings with her while he was masked, she would come to care for the man behind it.

The thought was foolish and self-delusional, but he let himself get lost for a few minutes in the fantasy. He didn't know why this particular woman had taken such a hold of him, but she'd become a fire in his blood he couldn't extinguish.

Erotic dreams haunted his nights, and he'd been unable to stay away from the theater. Tonight's encounter had only fueled his desire to know her better, to drown himself in her loveliness.

With a sigh, he poured himself a shot of whiskey and rang for Clinton. Tonight had been amazing, a perfect memory he could take to his grave, but he'd be an idiot to think he could ever repeat it.

* * * *

"Adrian!" The Earl of Hawkesmere's voice cracked like a whip in the silence of the quiet bedchamber.

Adrian startled awake, dropping the tumbler of whiskey he'd fallen asleep holding, then hissing in pain as the sudden movement disturbed his newly stitched wound.

"Who let you in?" he asked his older brother sullenly.

"Clinton sent word that you'd been shot," Lucien replied, crossing the room to Adrian's side. "My contact at Scotland Yard claims they almost caught you tonight. You're taking too many risks."

"I was always one step ahead of them," Adrian countered. "And I had some help." A tendril of warmth weaved its way through his chest as he thought of his beautiful guardian angel.

"What are you talking about?" Lucien asked suspiciously, sinking into the chair across from him.

"I was forced to take shelter with none other than Miss Vanessa Bourke."

"The actress?" Lucien shook his head. "What the hell were you thinking? I'm guessing you didn't end up there by accident. How did you even know where she lived?"

"You needn't worry," he told his brother, wishing he'd never mentioned the encounter. "She has no idea who I am."

"So what was she like?" Lucien asked, suddenly changing tactics.

"Lovelier than words can describe," Adrian replied a little wistfully, realizing with chagrin that he'd broached the subject out of an uncharacteristic need to talk about it. "She was frightened at first, to wake and find me there, but she recovered admirably, kept her head, and bandaged my wound. Then she let me kiss her."

Lucien frowned. "You do realize that by going to her as Prometheus, you've ruined your chances to get to know her as yourself."

Adrian laughed bitterly. "As if a woman like that would ever give my scarred face a second glance."

A flash of pain swept his brother's features. "You give yourself too little credit, brother. Perhaps you give the lady too little credit as well."

Adrian waved a dismissive hand. "Spare me the lecture."

With a sigh, Lucien pushed to his feet. "I'm glad to see you're all right, Adrian. Do try to be more careful in the future."

"Not bloody likely," Adrian whispered after his brother had exited the room. "Not very likely at all."

* * * *

Vanessa woke to find solemn blue eyes peering at her from mere inches away. As she stared into the little boy's wary face, the events of the previous evening came rushing back to her.

Prometheus had truly been here, in her bedroom, and he'd left this poor child he'd stolen from who knew what godforsaken den of iniquity behind.

He'd kissed her...

Before her mind could dwell too much on that particular topic, she pushed to her elbows and gave the boy a bright smile. "Good morning."

He continued to watch her but didn't reply. His stillness unnerved her a bit. She wondered sadly if he thought she was yet one more person who planned to hurt him. What was he supposed to think, when he woke to find himself in bed with a stranger?

"It's all right," she told him gently. "Prometheus brought you to me last night. He was shot in the leg when he was helping you escape. He feared he wouldn't be able to make it to the safe place he intended to take you, so he asked me to do it for him." As she said the words, a little shimmer of happiness went through her. Why had Prometheus come to her? How had he known he could trust her? She was determined not to let him down.

"Can you tell me your name?" she asked softly. He bit his lip, then ducked his head, still unresponsive. She wondered if he was mute or if he just didn't understand her. He had the wild, untamed beauty of a gypsy, with that curly dark hair, olive skin, and big blue eyes. With a sigh, she got out of bed and reached for her robe. Perhaps he'd feel more comfortable in the kitchen.

"My name is Vanessa," she told him. "There's a water closet down the hall if you need to use it. Then you can come find me in the kitchen, and we'll see if I can find anything worth eating."

He watched her for a moment longer, then slid out of bed and scampered down the hall. Not deaf then. And he obviously understood English. She tried not to be hurt that he chose not to speak to her. God only knew what he'd been through. Perhaps his silence was the only thing he felt he could control.

She wandered into the kitchen and perused her barren cupboards. She rarely ate at home, but she had picked up some sweet rolls last night from a street vendor. Not the best breakfast for a child, but she certainly hadn't planned on having one in her home this morning. She stoked a fire in the kitchen hearth so that she could make some hot chocolate, deciding they might as well be truly decadent.

After a few moments, she became aware of a presence behind her and turned to find the boy in the kitchen doorway, watching her as though she might reach out and strike him at any moment. She noticed he stood on the balls of his little feet, his whole body poised for flight.

"There's a sweet bun on the table." She forced a lightness to her voice she was far from feeling. "If you want to get started, go ahead. I'm making us some hot chocolate."

She turned her attention back to grating the chocolate and was pleased to see him inch forward in her peripheral vision.

"Prometheus wants me to take you to a place called Brookhaven," she continued, as though they were actually having a conversation. "It's an orphanage, but he assures me you'll be very well taken care of there. You'll never again have to do the things they made you do in that place he took you from."

He pulled out a chair and gracefully climbed into the seat, reaching tentatively for the bun, which he then wolfed down so quickly it left her wondering how long it had been since he'd last eaten.

Casually, she reached into the basket and handed him another. "It got me thinking though... Is there somewhere else you'd rather go? Do you have a family? Do you know how we can reach them?"

Perhaps he'd been stolen from a lovely home, though she knew enough of the world to doubt it. There were plenty of people who'd think nothing of selling their child into this life. He most likely was the son of a prostitute and had never known anything else.

When she met his unblinking gaze, he gave one emphatic shake of his head.

"No family," she murmured, to let him know she'd understood. Tears filled her eyes, and she blinked them hastily away. "That's all right, sweetheart. I promise I'll make sure this is a good place before I leave you there."

* * * *

Vanessa had rarely enjoyed an afternoon as much as she enjoyed the one she spent taking the boy to Brookhaven. She hired a hack, but they stopped to get sweets and a meat pie and ate them on the way. She kept up a running stream of banter with the child, and he warmed her heart by smiling shyly at her a few times, though he still hadn't spoken. She sensed he was still wary but cautiously optimistic that she didn't intend to hurt him. The resiliency of youth was quite amazing.

After nearly an hour in the hack, they pulled up in front of a huge, rambling white house with a wide expanse of green lawn. A dozen or more children played outside, and several matronly women watched over them.

Vanessa released a breath she hadn't realized she'd been holding. She'd feared Brookhaven would be something quite different, but she supposed she should have known Prometheus would not rescue these children from one hell, only to consign them to another.

"This 'ere's Brookhaven, miss," the hack driver informed her. "Will you be wantin' me to wait?"

"Yes, please," she told him. "I shouldn't be long."

She gave the boy a reassuring smile. "It looks very nice, doesn't it?"

He didn't reply, staring at his little feet with downcast eyes. With a sigh, she helped him down and led him through the gate.

A lovely young girl opened the front door just moments after Vanessa knocked. "May I help you, ma'am?"

"Hello," Vanessa said. "May I speak to whoever's in charge?"

"That would be Mrs. Bohannan," the girl informed her. "Right this way, please."

Vanessa and her small charge were led to a room at the back of the house, passing various classrooms and a large dining room along the way. The house had obviously been a private residence at one time and was very well taken care of. Everything was spotlessly clean and inviting.

Their guide poked her head in the room she'd led them to. "Visitors, Mrs. Bohannan."

"Show them in," came a soft, harried-sounding voice from within.

The girl gestured for them to enter.

To her surprise, Vanessa found that Mrs. Bohannan was very young, perhaps even younger than herself.

The lovely redhead was bent over a stack of ledgers, a pair of glasses perched upon the tip of her freckled nose. She glanced up as Vanessa entered, her green eyes immediately fixing upon the boy. "Hello," she said, a bit warily. "What can I do for you?"

"My name is Vanessa Bourke," Vanessa answered. "Prometheus asked me to bring this young man to you."

"Prometheus?" Mrs. Bohannan's eyebrows shot up in surprise. "He's never sent one of the children with someone else."

"He had little choice last night," Vanessa replied a bit defensively. "He'd been shot and didn't think he could make it himself."

"Shot?" Mrs. Bohannan got to her feet and circled her desk, her eyes filled with concern. "Is he all right?"

Vanessa nodded, wondering if this woman knew her masked midnight visitor's true identity. "I believe so. He was wounded in the leg, but I bandaged him up as well as I could."

Mrs. Bohannan openly sized Vanessa up. She probably had just as many questions about Vanessa's relationship with Prometheus as Vanessa had about hers. "How well do you know him?"

"How well do *you* know him?" Vanessa countered.

Mrs. Bohannan laughed and held her hands up in defeat. "I've never seen him without his mask if that's what you're asking."

Vanessa smiled wryly in return. "Neither have I."

They stared at each other for a moment longer, and then Mrs. Bohannan turned her attention back to the boy. "Hello there, young man," she murmured, dropping to her knees so she could look him in the eyes. "You're going to be very happy here. We'll take good care of you."

"He doesn't talk," Vanessa said when the boy didn't reply.

"A lot of them don't when they first arrive." Mrs. Bohannan gave him another smile, then got to her feet and stepped to the door. "Christina," she called.

Within moments, the girl who'd answered the door returned. "Yes, ma'am."

"Can you please take this young man up to the boy's floor and get him settled in? I need to talk with Miss Bourke a few moments more, and then I'll come up and see how he's doing."

"Of course." Christina smiled and held out a hand to the child. "Come with me."

He shook his head and buried his face in Vanessa's skirts.

Frowning, Vanessa knelt and hugged him tightly. "It will be all right," she whispered, stroking his soft, curly hair. "You're safe now, and if you like, I'll come and visit you."

He pulled back and gazed at her with heartbreaking trust.

She nodded, though he hadn't given voice to the question. "Yes, I promise. I will come and see you every chance I get."

He stared at her a moment longer, then turned toward Christina, squaring his little shoulders.

Vanessa watched him go, tears burning her eyes. She'd known him less than a day, yet the fierce concern and protectiveness she felt for the boy stunned her.

"I hope you meant that," Mrs. Bohannan told her with a sigh. "If you don't keep your promise, it will make it even harder for him."

"Of course I meant it," Vanessa replied, stung, even though she understood the other woman's concern. Truth be told, she'd made the offer impulsively, but she was determined to see it through. The boy needed her, and she'd never felt needed before.

Mrs. Bohannan returned to her chair. "Well, if you did mean it, you're more than welcome. You can come and see him any time."

"Thank you," Vanessa replied, her respect for this young woman growing with each passing moment. "I'll see you soon, then."

"I hope so," Mrs. Bohannan murmured, her attention already back on her books.

Chapter Three

Adrian stole down Brookhaven's hallway, shaking his head when he saw the light on in Fiona's office even though it was past midnight. Affection welled deep within him. Fiona had been the first one he'd rescued, and she had a special place in his heart. In the two years since he'd put her in charge of Brookhaven, she'd worked herself to the bone, her commitment to making a difference in the lives of these children even greater than his own, if such a thing was possible.

She'd taken to calling herself Mrs. Bohannan, though she'd never been married, in an attempt to make herself seem older. To him, she'd always be Fi, sixteen years old and sobbing as he rescued her from a house that specialized in men who liked to brutalize women.

Pausing outside her door, he self-consciously adjusted the mask. Foolish, he knew, to trust her with so much, yet keep this one part of himself a secret. It wasn't as though he feared her reaction to his scars. He'd kept her from learning his identity for purely practical reasons.

If anyone ever made the connection between Prometheus and the school, he wanted her to be able to maintain plausible deniability. Or at least that's what he told himself. Truth be told, he didn't think he could bear it if this woman ever looked at him with disgust. Or worse yet... pity.

"Burning the midnight oil again, Fi?" he asked softly as he entered the room.

She shot to her feet and launched herself into his arms, hugging him with surprising strength. "I've been so worried about you! Miss Bourke told me you'd been shot."

He let himself enjoy the rare embrace for a brief moment before stepping away. "I'm fine," he assured Fiona, settling into the chair that faced her desk. "Took a bullet in the leg, but it's healing nicely."

Truthfully, it hurt like the bloody devil. He'd been a fool to venture out tonight, only three days after it had happened, but he'd needed to make sure Miss Bourke hadn't disappointed him.

Fiona resumed her place behind the desk, shoving aside a stack of ledgers. "I was surprised when you sent the child with Miss Bourke. Wasn't sure whether to trust her. Perhaps we can work out some sort of password, in case you ever need to do such a thing again."

"Perhaps." He hid a smile, knowing how much Fiona loved being a part of the intrigue of his disguise and daring rescues. "In any event, it sounds as though she managed to get the boy here safely?"

Fiona nodded, giving him a considering look. "She's very lovely. I didn't take her seriously at first when she said the boy had taken hold of her heart. But she's come back to visit him every morning since she dropped him off, bringing him toys and clothes."

Adrian frowned at this unexpected news. Though he'd already held her in high esteem, he hadn't expected her to take an interest in the boy. "What do you think of her?" he asked pensively.

Fiona gave him an amused look. "She's beautiful, and she seems kind. Smart, too. I don't think she'll betray us. She cares too much for the boy."

"I'm glad to hear it," he said, relief sweeping through him. "I feared I'd made a mistake."

"It wouldn't hurt you to spread the load a little," Fiona told him, an old argument. "There are lots of people who'd be willing to help you with this, if you'd just let them."

"I have you," he reminded her, afraid to think too much about what Vanessa's visits meant, afraid to hope she might be everything she seemed.

"That you do." Fiona gave a bright, tinkling laugh. "I suppose the two of us can muck along alone. We've been doing it for a long time now, haven't we?"

"We have." He handed her a stack of cash, pushing all thoughts of Vanessa to the back of his mind. "Here's next month's expenses."

Fiona took the money with barely disguised relief. What a little bean counter she was. He provided plenty of funds to keep the house running, but she believed so passionately in what they were doing, and she was always afraid the well would run dry. He knew she worried that one day he'd be caught, and the funding would stop, even though he'd assured her that he'd made provisions for Brookhaven to continue, no matter what happened to him. His brothers contributed to this venture, though not as actively as he did, and they would never let it go under.

Unfortunately, Fiona had very little experience with men who kept their word.

"Well, I think I'll check in on our new arrival and then go home. I've been strictly forbidden to jump across rooftops for a few days, so it may be a while before you see me."

"Take care of yourself," Fiona said softly, as he turned toward the door. "There are a lot of people counting on you."

Her words created familiar tension within him. So many people counting on this charade. So many unfortunates still to rescue. For every one he saved, thousands continued to endure lives of slavery and pain. He couldn't stop, no matter how dangerous it became.

"He won't talk," Fiona called, as he stepped out into the hall. "We don't know his name."

He paused and glanced back, noticing that she was already back to her ledgers. "Get some sleep, Fi. That's an order."

She gave him a sheepish glance, but he continued staring at her until she shut the book and stood up. "All right. I'm going."

"Good girl," he muttered, as he headed toward the stairs. Fiona was only twenty-three. She shouldn't be saddled with so much responsibility, but she wouldn't have it any other way. She loved the children, and they loved her.

Once he reached the top floor, he moved quietly down the hall, looking in each open door, loving the soft chorus of snores. They slept four to a room, but the rooms were snug and warm, the beds clean and comfortable. He stopped at the last room on the right, where the youngest boys were housed. His most recent rescue slept peacefully in one of the beds, his inky hair a striking contrast to the crisp white pillow.

Adrian stared down at the boy for a long moment, letting deep satisfaction well within him. This was why he did it. So children like this one could have a childhood filled with good memories that would hopefully wipe out the darkness that came before.

* * * *

Adrian slid open Vanessa's third-floor window, grimacing at the strain on his injured leg as he quietly swung through. He'd meant to go straight home after leaving Brookhaven, but he'd found himself coming here again instead.

He couldn't stop thinking about what Fiona had said. Why hadn't Vanessa simply dropped the boy off and gone back to her glamorous life? Why would a woman like her spend hours playing with children at an orphanage? He needed to find the answer to that question. He had to see her again.

Smoothing his hand over the mask, he made sure it was still in place. As long as he wore it he could be himself, without feeling self-conscious. For the first time in his life, he had the opportunity to interact with a beautiful woman without the distraction of his scars.

He stood for a moment just inside the window, letting his eyes grow accustomed to the darkness, listening for the sound of Vanessa's soft breathing. When he determined that she was indeed in the room, he crossed the heavy carpet to her side. The bedclothes rustled as she suddenly scrambled to a sitting position.

"Don't be afraid," he hastened to reassure her. "It's just me."

"Just you?" She gave a soft, incredulous laugh. "By that you mean, 'just the masked villain who already broke into my room and scared me to death once before'?"

A smile curved his lips at her sassy tone. The girl had spunk; he'd give her that. And it felt good to smile. He couldn't remember the last time he'd done so out of genuine pleasure. "Yes," he murmured. "Just that masked villain."

"Why did you come back?" Despite her attempted bravery, a trace of apprehension laced her voice, and guilt surged through him.

"I'll leave if you wish. I just... wanted to see you again."

Silence fell between them, and his heart sank. Of course, she didn't want him here. He'd been a fool to think she'd welcome him back with the same sweet passion she'd shown before. He spun on his heels, heading back the way he'd come.

"How is your leg?"

He paused and turned slowly back, straining to see her face in the dark. "On the mend."

"You shouldn't even be on your feet," she chided softly. "Come. Sit down beside me and rest for a while before you leave."

Her offer made him think of the Christmas mornings of his childhood. Before his father had died. Before he'd been burned. When he'd still believed anything was possible.

As he crossed the room, he flicked on the gas, illuminating the room in soft light. He sank stiffly onto the edge of her bed, breathing deeply as her feminine scent enveloped him. Vanilla and a light hint of cinnamon. Warm, homey smells, not the heavy floral perfume he'd expected.

"Is the mask really necessary?"

"I don't want to put you at risk," he asserted, sickness blooming in the pit of his stomach at the thought of facing her without the safety of his disguise.

"I read about what you did the other night. It was very foolish. Why do you take such risks?"

For a moment, he considered telling her the truth. What was it about this woman that made him such a stranger to himself? Never before had he felt the urge to reveal himself in such a way. "Someone has to do it," he answered vaguely instead. "I like doing it."

She shook her head with a faint smile. "I'm used to narcissistic actors. Altruistic behavior confounds me, but I find it refreshing. And admirable."

Beneath the mask, heat burned his cheeks at her unexpected praise. "My actions are far from altruistic, I can assure you. I do it less for those unfortunate wretches I rescue than from the need to destroy the evil men who prey on the weak and innocent."

She leaned toward him and squeezed his hand. "You're a hero in my eyes. I don't care about your motives."

He twined his fingers with hers, not such a hero that he wasn't fully prepared to take advantage of her misconceptions. "You've haunted me since I last saw you. I haven't been able to stop thinking of you."

"I've thought about you, too," she admitted with a half-smile. "I'm glad you came back. I was afraid I wouldn't see you again."

Her words thrilled him, but he stopped himself from saying something about that kiss. He didn't want to scare her away or for her to think he'd come here with thoughts of getting another one, even though he wanted nothing more.

"I hear you've been visiting the boy," he said instead. "Fiona says you've been there every day."

She nodded, her eyes sparkling with obvious affection. "He's such an amazing child. I wish I could take him in, but the life of an actress is not suited for raising children."

He heard an underlying note of bitterness. "Was your mother an actress?"

"My father was an actor. He and my mother were never married, so I never even met him until she died." She released his hand and folded her slim arms defensively, obviously unsure how he would take the news that she was a bastard. "He had no idea how to be a parent. He left me in dressing rooms and empty flats, forgot about me completely more often than not. I would never want that for a child of my own."

He wished she hadn't let go of his hand. He wanted to offer her comfort. "Don't say such things," he chided gently. "You're not your father. The boy thinks the world of you. I'm sure you'd be a wonderful mother."

Her dark eyes sparkled with a sheen of tears, which she quickly blinked away. "Thank you. I hope so. One day, perhaps."

"One day," he repeated, throwing caution to the wind and once again reaching for her hand. She surrendered it reluctantly, still rather defensive. He sensed she hadn't volunteered so much to anyone in quite some time and still wasn't sure why she'd opened up to him. He couldn't imagine why she'd chosen to trust him, but her story touched him deeply.

He twined his fingers with hers and squeezed her hand. "When I watched you on stage, I was certain you loved being an actress."

She shrugged, dropping her gaze. "It's my job to make you think that. But in truth, I hate the uncertainty, the lack of stability. I've lived in this flat for two years, and that's the longest

I've ever stayed in one place in my life. All I want is a home, a family..." She trailed off in embarrassment.

"Any man would be glad to start a family with you," he told her in a hushed voice, wishing he could be that man.

She cleared her throat. "I wish you'd take off that mask. Maybe it's the anonymity that has allowed me to talk to you this way, but it's a little disconcerting."

He lifted his hand, automatically checking to make sure the fabric hadn't shifted. "I'm sorry, Miss Bourke. I can't take that risk."

Her face fell, and he knew he'd disappointed her. "I understand," she said, but it was obvious that she didn't. She'd opened herself up to him and apparently hoped he would do so in return. But he wouldn't. He couldn't. He didn't even know if he knew how.

"I should go," he said abruptly, wondering why the hell he'd come. He could never have a real relationship with this woman. Not with the mask and definitely not without it.

"Don't go," she told him, tightening her grip on his hand briefly before letting go. "I'm sorry if I said something wrong. You don't have to take off the mask."

"It's nothing you did," he assured her, getting to his feet and trying to hide his wince when he put his weight on his wounded leg. "I never should have come here. It's not safe for either of us. I just wanted to say thank you, for all you did for me and the child."

"You're welcome," she whispered as he turned to the window. "Will I see you again?"

He hesitated but didn't turn around. "I don't know."

He hoped not. He hoped he had the strength to stay away.

IF YOU'D LIKE TO READ MORE, YOU CAN FIND THE FULL VERSION OF THIS BOOK FOR FREE ON MOST EBOOK RETAILERS, INCLUING AMAZON, BARNES & NOBLE, APPLE iBOOKS, GOOGLE PLAY, AND KOBO.

GAMBLING ON THE DUKE'S DAUGHTER
Chapter One

London, 1867

The Earl of Warren's London townhouse stood in fashionable Grosvenor Square. The Palladian monstrosity with its imposing white columns had been in the Blake family for generations. On this particular May evening, every window blazed with light, even though dawn would break in a matter of hours.

Dylan Blake, the earl's youngest son, paid the driver of the hired hack that had brought him and alighted from the vehicle with a jaunty step. His black velvet cloak whipped in the chill spring breeze, and the solid weight of his dress sword bumped against his thigh. He strode toward the red brick mansion that had never felt like a home with rebellion in his heart.

Half a dozen footmen in deep blue livery waited on the front steps, their faces impassive as they shivered in the cold. One of the young men bowed deeply and hurried to open the door, letting the festive sounds of laughter and music drift out into the night. Dylan grinned at the lad as he crossed the threshold.

The midnight supper had ended but plenty of guests remained for the dancing. His timing couldn't have been better.

The butler, Wadsworth, lifted a disapproving brow as Dylan entered, but the old man was too well-trained to chide his employee's son for his late arrival. "Shall I announce you, sir?"

Dylan nodded, his blood pounding with the thrill of having thwarted one of his father's plans. Childish, he knew, to continually provoke the man, but sometimes he just couldn't help himself.

Surrendering his cloak to one of the footmen, Dylan followed the aging butler up the grand staircase with its intricately carved banisters, then down the long hall that led to the ballroom. He was dressed for effect tonight in his scarlet military regalia, his medals and gold epaulets flashing in the candlelight. They passed several aristocratic guests along the way, but Dylan ignored their stares and whispers.

The heady scents of beeswax and roses assaulted his senses as he entered the ballroom. The laughter and buzz of conversation indicated the earl's privileged guests were having a good time.

Dylan scanned the crowd, his smile widening. He hadn't been to one of these affairs in more than a decade, but nothing had changed. Society girls in elaborate gowns still whirled around the parquet dance floor on the arms of suitable young gentlemen. Titled matrons still schemed and plotted from the corners as the older men congregated in small groups, looking bored.

When the last notes of the current waltz faded away, Wadsworth cleared his throat. "The Honorable Captain Dylan Blake."

For a moment, utter silence reigned. Scores of interested nobles craned their necks for a glimpse of the earl's prodigal son, home at last after twelve long years of dedicated service to the Crown.

Dylan met his father's furious gaze. He smiled, then turned his back and skirted the gleaming dance floor. *Let the old bastard come to me.* His days of seeking the old man's favor were long past.

After an awkward pause, the music started up again, as did the whispers.

Julian Tremaine, Lord Basingstoke, who was Dylan's only friend in this whole crowd, strode toward him. Dressed in austere black, as usual, the earl's eyes glinted with welcome. "Blake! Where the hell have you been?"

Dylan shrugged, amused by the knowledge that everyone else wanted to know the same thing. "I had a prior engagement."

Basingstoke stared at him for a moment, then chuckled in admiration. "You were with Cassandra, weren't you?" He shook his head in astonishment. "Has there ever been a woman you *couldn't* get, once you set your mind to it?"

"Never." Dylan grabbed a glass of champagne from a passing waiter and took a long, appreciative drink. "It's the uniform. Besides, I'm making up for lost time. I was in the Army for a bloody long time, you know."

Basingstoke laughed, then sobered and nodded in Warren's direction. "Well, I hope she was worth it. Your father was furious when you didn't show up for dinner. Threw off the whole thing. Uneven number, and all that."

Exactly one hundred of London's most elite and fashionable attended Warren's annual ball. Because of its exclusivity, the *ton* considered an invitation to be the height of social accomplishment.

The earl had debated long and hard about allowing his younger son to attend. By selling out early in his career, Dylan had taken the place of some far more deserving social climber. The earl had lectured Dylan endlessly about the importance of the occasion and threatened vague, dire consequences should Dylan do anything beyond the pale.

For these reasons and a thousand more, Dylan had taken a sinful amount of pleasure in the fact that his late arrival had turned his father's One Hundred Ball into a dinner of ninety-nine.

There would be hell to pay for this latest transgression, but Dylan was enjoying the moment anyway.

"My father has been furious with me since the day I was born," he told Basingstoke with a shrug. "I figured I might as well give him a reason."

Out of the corner of his eye, Dylan saw his older brother, Michael, confer with the earl, then move through the crowd in Dylan's direction.

As blond and golden as Adonis, Michael had always been the earl's pride and joy. Viscount Sherbourne from birth, Michael would one day inherit the earldom and all the wealth and privilege that went with it. In return, Michael kept his reputation above reproach and obeyed their father's every command.

No doubt he was obeying one of those commands now.

"Let's go down to the billiard room." Dylan refused to stick around and be chastened in such a civilized manner. He'd much prefer it if his father made a scene and took him to task for his irresponsible behavior once and for all.

But that would never happen. The earl didn't care enough about his second son to expend such emotion.

* * *

"He's a disgrace! Honestly, can you believe the nerve! Making a scene and ruining a perfectly lovely ball!" Lady Amelia Lansdowne fluttered her filigreed fan with unusual vigor, an unbecoming flush on her pale cheeks.

"I wouldn't call this a scene, Amelia. He merely arrived a little late. I'm sure he had a good reason." Lady Natalia Sinclair sighed with impatience over her companion's melodrama, but her own fan fluttered a bit faster as she watched Captain Blake chat with Lord Basingstoke.

Captain Dylan Blake, recipient of the Victoria's Cross.

Natalia knew all about him. She'd read dozens of newspaper articles touting his courage, but she'd never actually met him.

"He's dreadfully good-looking," she mused, as she cast a subtle glance in the captain's direction.

In his scarlet dress uniform, with his confident military bearing and chest full of medals, he stood out in the crowd of somber, black-garbed lords. His thick black hair, caught at his nape with a piece of scarlet ribbon, contrasted sharply with his light blue eyes. His high, chiseled cheekbones, square jaw, and clear, sun-kissed skin stole her breath.

Amelia gave a delicate shudder. "How can you say such a thing? He hasn't a title nor a farthing to his name. He's been in the military for years, serving with the very dregs of society, and probably doesn't know the first thing about how to act around civilized people."

"Surely, the fact that he fought to preserve our way of life gives him the right to a few eccentricities. He's a hero, Amelia."

Natalia didn't bother to point out that a man's wealth had nothing to do with how attractive he was. It wouldn't do any good. In Amelia's eyes, money and power *did* determine a man's worth.

Unfortunately, Natalia's father shared Amelia's opinions, and he would choose her future husband.

Amelia turned up her nose with a condescending sniff. "Well, hero or not, you wouldn't catch *me* marrying such a man."

"No." Natalia fought to maintain a civil tone. "I don't suppose so." *Not that a hero like Captain Blake would want to marry a little cat like you anyway.*

To her relief, Amelia soon drifted away, obviously in search of someone more inclined to share her narrow-minded opinions. Natalia found herself alone for a few moments, free to daydream about Captain Blake.

She wanted to meet him, even though her father would never permit a man like Captain Blake to court her. It seemed so unfair. What good were wealth and a title, when so many of those who had them lacked even a hint of character?

Captain Blake had risked his life to save his men. He'd dashed back into the fray three times before he'd been wounded. The mere thought of his courageous actions sent a shiver down her spine.

Unfortunately, Captain Blake and Lord Basingstoke left the ballroom before she could work up the audacity to arrange an introduction. Disappointed, Natalia forced a smile as the next young man on her dance card claimed her for a mazurka.

Lord Roger Densby was the son of a duke. While undoubtedly her social equal, he was at least two stones overweight and stank of sweat and brandy.

He managed to step on her toes twice before he even got her out on the dance floor and didn't have a heroic bone in his entire well-fed body.

Densby, or someone like him, was her fate. Still, her entire soul rebelled at the thought of spending her life with a man who wasn't interested in anything but the next hunt or glittering party.

What she really wanted was someone like Captain Blake—a man with poetry in his face and courage in his heart.

Chapter Two

At least a dozen of London's most eligible bachelors occupied the Earl of Warren's posh, walnut-paneled billiard room. Some lounged on deep leather chairs, immersed in card games, while others stood around the billiard table, wagering on everything from who would sink the next shot to who would win the next Derby. Here they were free to drink, smoke, and gamble away from the censorious eyes of prospective mothers-in-law.

Dylan had spent a fair amount of time with this crowd, out of sheer boredom and disillusionment, but, save Basingstoke, he didn't like or respect any of them. They reminded him of a flock of squawking crows, circling restlessly as they waited to come into the wealth and position they hadn't earned and didn't deserve.

Unfortunately, his own days were just as meaningless.

He'd sold his commission in hopes his father would allow him to take over the management of one of the many estates entailed to the Blake family. He'd wanted the peace of England's lush green hills. Homesickness had consumed him during those last endless months in the Army.

But he should have known his father would never allow him to have what he wanted. The earl met his request with incredulous laughter, and nothing came of his subsequent attempts to find such work on his own. No one believed the son of an earl, even a second son with no money or prospects, actually wanted to get his hands dirty.

Was his need for peace and tranquility so hard to understand? All he wanted was a quiet place to lick a decade's worth of wounds.

"Well, well," Lord Jonathan Taylor drawled, as Dylan and Basingstoke took seats at a table in a secluded corner of the room. "Look who finally managed to put in an appearance."

Jonathan had been picking fights with Dylan since they were in short pants, and he was already well in his cups, his pale eyes glittering with animosity.

The little bugger is in fine form tonight. Dylan suppressed a weary sigh and accepted another drink from a nearby waiter. The thrill of thwarting his father had worn off. He'd need plenty of liquid fortification in order to get through the rest of the evening.

"I know where he's been." Viscount Harding, one of Dylan's old schoolmates, winked before he sank a ball in the far pocket. "I saw him with Cassandra Lockhart this afternoon."

Basingstoke chuckled and quaffed his drink. "He's a master, gentlemen. I've yet to see a woman who didn't succumb to his charms."

Jonathan gave a derisive laugh. "I'm not impressed. Miss Lockhart is an actress. What sport is there in that?"

Quite a lot, actually, since Cassandra was the actress in question. The fiery redhead had taken London's theater set by storm. Every man in this room had tried to seduce her, but she'd refused all suitors until Dylan had charmed his way into her bed earlier this evening.

Dylan gave Jonathan a measuring look. "Do you have a more challenging target in mind? Your sister, perhaps?" He knew he was being obnoxious, but Jonathan's last taunt had hit a nerve. The endless couplings with actresses and high-priced courtesans left him empty.

Jonathan's homely, sharp-featured face flushed with anger. His older sister resembled a horse and had been on the shelf for years, despite her distinguished family name. "Take it back, Blake, or I swear I *will* call you out this time."

Dylan shrugged. "Name your second."

"Now, gentlemen," Basingstoke interceded, ever the mediator. Jonathan had challenged Dylan to at least a dozen duels in the past. "We're all friends here. I don't think it needs to come to that."

Viscount Harding drifted near enough to hear the gist of the conversation and clapped his hand on Jonathan's thin shoulder. "Think about what you're saying, old chap. Blake is a bloody national hero. He's killed dozens of men. Do you really want to be added to that number?"

With seething impatience, Dylan waited for Jonathan to make up his mind. He wouldn't kill the little fop. Harding was right—enough blood stained his hands.

At last, Jonathan seemed to realize the odds were against him. He glared at Dylan with unconcealed hatred. "Perhaps you'd like to make a wager, instead? Your somewhat dubious charms against a woman of my choosing?"

Dylan ignored the low rumble of excited whispers their little scene had provoked. He didn't understand why Jonathan took Dylan's every victory as a personal defeat. "I don't gamble on women. Besides, Cassandra and I have barely begun our liaison."

But he thought of the emptiness he'd felt even in Cassandra's most intimate embrace and knew he wouldn't bother to see her again.

"Afraid you'll lose?" Jonathan mocked. "Afraid no decent woman will have you?"

At this little bit of absurdity, Dylan laughed outright. "Why on earth would I want a respectable woman? If I go sniffing around one of them, I'll end up married to the chit."

Basingstoke raised a brow and gave Dylan a wry smile. "And what would be the harm in that? A big fat dowry is exactly what you need."

Unfortunately, Basingstoke knew the way of it. Nine months of high living had depleted the funds Dylan had received for selling his commission. Actresses might be easy, but they weren't cheap.

Soon, he'd be forced to ask his father for an increase of his pitiful quarterly stipend. Anything would be better than that, even marriage.

Perhaps this foolish bet could stave off that necessity for a little while longer.

"All right," Dylan murmured. "Who is it to be, then? I've always wanted to make a good girl go bad."

Jonathan stepped a little closer and lowered his voice, so only Dylan, Basingstoke, and Harding could hear. "How about Lady Natalia Sinclair?"

"Out of the question!" Basingstoke shook his head and flashed Dylan a warning glance. "Don't even think about it, Blake."

Unnecessary advice. Even Dylan had heard of the fair Lady Natalia.

The Duke of Clayton's daughter had an enormous dowry, perhaps half a million pounds. But she'd cut through the men who tried to court her like a knife through butter.

Given Jonathan's simmering anger, Dylan guessed he'd felt the sting of her rejection. The bet suddenly made sense. Jonathan wanted to see Dylan fail.

Although Lady Natalia might be a worthy adversary, Dylan wasn't foolish enough to trifle with the duke's daughter. Clayton was one of the most powerful men in Britain and would never allow his daughter anywhere near a penniless younger son.

"Have you seen her?" Jonathan persisted.

Dylan shook his head. He'd tried to steer clear of this kind of social event since his return. Besides, he had no interest in the marriage-minded young women who populated London's exclusive drawing rooms.

Not that a woman like Lady Natalia Sinclair would have been within reach, even if he had been looking.

"Give it a try," Jonathan urged. "I'll make it easy on you. All you need to do is get her to agree to a second dance, a boon she has yet to grant anyone. One hundred pounds if you succeed."

One hundred pounds. It was a small fortune, and Dylan badly needed the funds.

He'd much rather dance with some silly young girl than beg his father for an advance. Especially given his behavior tonight.

"All right," Dylan agreed. "You're on."

* * *

Natalia spent the next hour sending covert glances toward the ballroom entrance, hoping for another tantalizing glimpse of Captain Blake. She refused to believe he'd already left. Who knew if she'd ever cross paths with him again?

Just when she'd nearly given up hope, she caught sight of his brilliant scarlet uniform. Her heart gave a little thrill of delight. Perhaps she'd have a chance to meet him, after all.

Unfortunately, Captain Blake accompanied Lord Jonathan Taylor, one of her most annoying and persistent suitors. Usually, she dissuaded unwanted attention with a condescending stare, but Lord Jonathan had not yet taken the hint.

She wondered what the little weasel had in common with a hero like Captain Blake. Surely, they weren't friends?

The two men spoke intently for a few moments, but to her relief, Lord Jonathan soon drifted away, leaving Captain Blake alone. Perfect. She was breathless with excitement at this unexpected stroke of luck.

The next man on her dance card arrived, and Natalia sent him off to fetch a glass of champagne. Having bought herself another moment or two of solitude, she plotted her next move. How could she arrange an introduction to the captain without damaging her reputation?

The captain remained at the edge of the crowd, leaning against one of the marble pillars as he cast his brooding gaze over the assembled guests. His thick, inky black hair made a stark contrast to the white stone, and his broad shoulders spanned the entire width of the column.

To her everlasting embarrassment, he caught her staring. One corner of his mouth lifted in a questioning smile, and his disturbing blue gaze met hers with shocking familiarity. A strange little quiver raced up and down her spine.

He'd been the main topic of conversation during the past hour, and everything she'd heard only intrigued her more. Dylan Blake was one of her peers, yet he'd chosen to break free of the stifling restraints aristocratic society placed on its members.

Ever since he'd sold his commission and returned to London, he'd refused to conform to his father's wishes. Rumor had it that his father had been furious with him for selling out and had refused his request to give him an estate of his own to manage.

Undaunted, Captain Blake had begun searching for work as an estate manager somewhere else, a quest nobody could understand. A gentleman did *not* work. It simply wasn't done.

In response to his scandalous actions, the *ton* had closed ranks against him. None of them would allow him to manage so much as a haystack.

But Natalia approved of his need to do something worthwhile. How could anyone expect a man who had done such great things, who was used to being in command, to come back to England and rest on his laurels?

The other rumors concerned her a little more, given her intense attraction to the man. Apparently, he was a rake and a womanizer, but Natalia decided those were small things, easily forgiven in light of the fact that he'd spent the last twelve years fighting for his country.

Perhaps all he needed was the right woman. Someone who would love him enough to calm his restless spirit. She desperately wanted to talk to him. She needed to prove to herself that the man she'd idolized for so long was worthy of her affections.

Something good and fine lurked behind that too-handsome face and mocking smile; she just knew it.

Unfortunately, she still hadn't figured out how to initiate a conversation with him.

For the Duke of Clayton's daughter, the world was a narrow and confining place. Soon, her father would decide on a suitable husband, and, after her marriage, she'd be sent away to some country pile to produce the requisite heir and spare. Her own wants and wishes didn't matter.

Still, she couldn't resist glancing at Dylan Blake again and again. Why did he keep looking at her? From everything she'd heard, she didn't think he cared about marriage.

Surely, he realized her father would never consider him?

Her gaze met his once more and a ripple of awareness sent shockwaves through her very heart. The duke might not consider Dylan Blake suitable, but she found him absolutely perfect. More than handsome, he embodied all her dangerous dreams.

As though he'd read her mind and knew how much she wanted to meet him, he smiled and moved toward her through the crowd. She watched, torn between terror and heady excitement as he paused to speak to her cousin, Nigel Sinclair. Nigel frowned a bit, then nodded, and the two men headed her way.

As they approached, Nigel gave her an apologetic little smile, as though on a distasteful but necessary mission. She clenched her fists, and her nails bit into her palms as she struggled to keep her emotions in check. She shouldn't want this introduction so badly and must never allow her true feelings to show.

"Lady Natalia Sinclair, allow me to introduce Captain Dylan Blake." Nigel smiled at her again, as though the two of them shared a private joke at the expense of the earl's prodigal son.

Captain Blake smiled as well, drawing her gaze to the lush, full curve of his lips, so at odds with the harsh, uncompromising line of his jaw. His dark lashes, too, seemed out of place. The thick fringe framed his eyes in a sensuous tangle.

And the impact of that stare up close took her breath away. His eyes weren't really blue, she discovered. They were gray, the color of smoke and stormy skies.

He bowed with effortless grace and then brought her gloved hand to his lips. The heat of his mouth warmed her skin through the thin layer of silk. "Lady Natalia." His voice was smooth and cultured, as beautiful as the rest of him. "It's a pleasure to make your acquaintance."

Unsettled and strangely breathless, she forced herself to hide her unusual attack of nerves. "Good evening, Captain Blake."

Ever since her debut, men had thronged to her side in hopes of winning her dowry. She'd learned early to protect herself, to be cool and cutting and utterly unimpressed with the many insincere words her suitors lavished upon her. As a result, London's young rakes thought her cold and haughty.

She took a certain amount of pleasure in that.

It wouldn't do to let Dylan Blake know he'd melted all her defenses with one burning glance in her direction.

"Would you do me the honor of the next dance?" His smile dazzled her, even though it was practiced and didn't quite reach those spectacular eyes.

But something in his tone, in the falseness of that wicked grin, gave her pause. She looked deep into those silver-gray eyes and found... nothing. No answering spark of attraction, no emotion whatsoever. For such a young man, his eyes were incredibly old. Dead.

In fact, she had the feeling he didn't really see her at all.

Disappointment lanced through her. She'd thought him a hero, but he was no different than the rest. She was a dowry, a prize to be won, nothing more. Certainly not a real person, with hopes and dreams of her own.

When he looked at her, all he saw was a way of financing an estate of his own.

She hated him suddenly, hated him for making her want him when he felt nothing in return.

"I'm sorry, Captain Blake, but my dance card is full." She gave him her most wintry stare, the one intended to put him in his place.

His look of astonishment was almost comical. Apparently—and not surprisingly—he'd had little experience with feminine rejection.

"Of course. My mistake." Giving her another graceful bow, he pivoted and strode off through the crowd.

"What an insufferable boor." Nigel tossed her a superior grin. "Well done, Nat. You certainly let him know the way of things."

Natalia ignored her cousin's inane chatter. As she watched Captain Blake walk away, she wished with all her heart that he'd stayed on the other side of the ballroom. Far better for him to have remained a beautiful fantasy than to have learned the truth.

Dylan Blake was not the answer to her prayers.

He was just another fortune hunter—one who hadn't even pretended to like her for something other than her dowry.

Chapter Three

"I need two more weeks," Dylan told Jonathan as they exited the ballroom. "You can't expect me to win her over in two minutes."

Jonathan laughed, the sour sound tinged with satisfaction. "It wouldn't matter if I gave you a year. Lady Natalia will never want what little you have to offer."

Dylan said nothing. Lady Natalia's dismissal had left him reeling.

When Jonathan first pointed her out, Dylan thought the whole thing would be ridiculously easy. She'd seemed transfixed by him, breathless with yearning.

But when he'd asked her to dance, the light had gone out of her lovely green eyes. She'd become every bit as cold and condescending as he'd heard.

Needless to say, the challenge she presented made her infinitely more appealing. Besides, he couldn't afford to lose this bet with Jonathan. He didn't have one hundred pounds to give the bastard.

"Two more weeks," he bargained. "And we'll double the wager. Two hundred pounds if I lose."

Jonathan thought it over for half a second and then nodded. "All right. Two hundred pounds. But you'd better be good for it."

"I'm good for it," Dylan lied.

"Excellent. Then it's settled." Jonathan's wide smile seemed out of place on his pinched little face. "Shall we have another drink?"

Dylan shook his head and glanced toward the stairs that led to the family's private rooms. He had no desire to return to the party. "No, you go ahead. I'm off to bed."

Turning his back on Jonathan, Dylan made his way through the deserted upper floors of his father's house to the suite of rooms he seldom used.

Lady Natalia presented an intriguing puzzle.

She was nothing he'd expected her to be. Young, yes. But not silly or simpering. Her looks were far too striking to be fashionable, but he'd never cared much for the pale, willowy blondes who were all the rage.

The top of the tiny brunette's head didn't even reach his chin, and her demure white gown did nothing to hide her voluptuous curves. Her mother, the duke's first wife, had been a Russian princess. Perhaps that accounted for the exotic tilt of those wide, emerald eyes, and the full lush mouth he'd instantly imagined kissing.

He let himself into his old room and sank down on the huge pedestal bed. Loosening his cravat, he stared into the empty grate, still trying to make sense of what had gone wrong.

He'd thought her pretty at first sight, exquisite up close. But when she'd stared deep into his eyes—and he'd noticed the passion and light fade from hers—she'd become more than just a quick way to make a hundred pounds.

Since his return to London, no one else had made an effort to see behind the careful façade he'd erected to keep the world at bay. Unfortunately, he had the distinct impression that what she'd seen had disappointed her in some soul-deep way.

If she'd caught even a glimpse of the things he kept hidden, it was no wonder. Ugliness seethed within him. It seemed a farce that God had gifted him with such a pleasing form and face. Then again, Lucifer had been the most beautiful of all the angels.

"What did you see, Natalia?" he whispered into the stillness of the room. And he wondered why he cared.

* * *

The Earl of Warren's ball seemed to last forever. Natalia went through the motions. She smiled and danced as though having the time of her life, but in truth, her feet were killing her, and she was desperate for the evening to end.

As she fended off Lord Jonathan Taylor's advances for the dozenth time—and earned a fulminating glare from the gentleman in question—she wished for the peace and quiet of her father's country estate. Now that she saw the reality of Town life, she couldn't imagine why she'd been so excited to make her debut.

The Season was only a few weeks old, but she'd already grown tired of the constant social whirl. The endless balls, teas, concerts, and soirees exhausted her.

It might have been different if she'd been allowed her to choose her own husband, but she knew she wouldn't have any say in the matter. Her father would choose for her, and there wasn't a single thing she could do about it.

Why take the time to get to know any of the young men who flocked to her side? If she foolishly fell in love, she'd only wind up with a broken heart.

She felt like a fraud, a carrot her father dangled in front of London's most eligible bachelors for the contrary satisfaction of snatching her away. It was a game to him.

She suspected he'd already struck a deal with one of her mother's Russian cousins. No ordinary earl or marquess would do. No. The duke's daughter would marry a prince.

As a matter of fact, when the Season ended, the duke intended to take Natalia to St. Petersburg for a prolonged visit with Prince Nikolai Ivanovich.

The duke assured Natalia nothing was definite. He claimed she'd have the chance to get to know Prince Nikolai before he agreed to the marriage. But she'd already met the prince, long ago, and had no desire to further their acquaintance.

Nikolai was handsome, but calculated cruelty lay in the depths of his ice-blue eyes. The mere thought of becoming his wife made her uneasy.

Her father refused to listen to her fears. She'd been a child the last time she and Nikolai met, he reminded her. She needed to give the prince a chance, see him with the eyes of a woman.

In response, she'd tried to make herself unapproachable, going so far as to deny any man the privilege of more than one dance a night. She didn't want to encourage anyone unduly, didn't want to make any of these young men think they had a chance at winning her hand and, more importantly, the fortune that came with it.

"I believe this last dance is mine."

The gentleman who'd spoken approached when Natalia's former partner—an elderly German count, who'd trampled on her toes—led her off the dance floor. The handsome newcomer, with his golden hair and deep blue eyes, looked familiar.

Natalia smiled with more enthusiasm than she'd shown all evening. The last dance. *Finally*.

She glanced down at her dance card, and then back at her new partner with renewed interest. "Lord Sherbourne?" Michael Blake, the Earl of Warren's heir—and Captain Blake's older brother.

Sherbourne nodded. Genuine warmth sparkled in his eyes. "I've been looking forward to this dance all evening, Lady Natalia."

"You flatter me, Lord Sherbourne." The practiced words slipped easily off her tongue. For once, she allowed herself to relax and be a little flirtatious. It was late, and she grew tired of guarding her heart.

The string quartet began yet another waltz. To her delight, Sherbourne danced divinely. As they whirled across the thinning dance floor, she took the opportunity to study him and marveled at his lack of resemblance to the captain. She would never have known they were related, if not for their names.

Unfortunately, Sherbourne came up lacking.

Sherbourne was a bit shorter and thinner than his younger brother, and his warm blue eyes weren't as intense. Nothing mysterious or rebellious about this man. In fact, she'd bet a million pounds he'd done exactly what was expected of him his entire life.

He was titled, wealthy, and handsome—everything Society found attractive in a man. So, why didn't he have the same effect on her that his brother did? In Sherbourne's arms, she felt none of the rioting emotions Captain Blake elicited with one casual glance.

"It's been a wonderful party." Afraid Sherbourne might somehow read her wayward thoughts, she kept up a steady stream of small talk. "Your father is a magnificent host."

Sherbourne gave a short laugh. "I'm just glad it's over. If I never see another guest list in my life, it will be too soon." His candor surprised her. Perhaps she'd been wrong, and there was a bit of rebelliousness behind his blandly perfect features. She wanted to commiserate, tell him of her own impatience with the endless rounds of invitations, but years of training kept the words locked in her throat.

Before she could think of anything else to say, the music died away. Sherbourne released her with obvious reluctance. "The dance was much too short. Perhaps you would allow me to call on you tomorrow?"

Such a simple request, but she'd yet to grant such favor to any of her suitors. Her first impulse was to refuse him, as she'd done all the others. But thoughts of the foolish way she'd behaved over his sinfully attractive brother stayed her tongue.

Perhaps, she'd refused the others because she'd secretly been searching for a hero, *someone to love* all along. Somehow, she'd turned Captain Blake into such a paragon of virtue in her mind that no one, not even the captain himself, could live up to her imaginings.

If so, she truly was a fool. Far better to play the game and continue to guard her heart.

"I'd like that," she told Sherbourne. "I'd like that very much."

* * *

By the time Dylan entered the dining room the next morning, every trace of the party had been swept away. A sideboard of delicacies gave off assorted tantalizing smells, and his stomach growled noisily.

He'd missed dinner, after all.

Michael entered the room while Dylan filled his plate. They eyed each other warily. The easy friendship they'd enjoyed as children had disappeared long ago.

"Good morning," Dylan said, hoping to set a light tone. He wasn't in the mood to argue or to be lectured. He wanted to eat and then make his exit before his father showed up.

"Hello." Michael sounded surprised by his pleasant greeting. "I didn't know you'd spent the night."

It was a good beginning. Dylan couldn't even remember the last time he and his brother had managed to carry on a conversation not marred by anger, jealousy, or defensiveness.

"I stayed for breakfast." Dylan sat down at one end of the huge walnut table and dug into his kippers with relish. "You can't get fare like this down at Mrs. Tweed's."

Michael filled his own plate and then took the place across from Dylan, frowning. "You don't have to live in that deuced boarding house, you know. You're welcome to come home anytime you wish."

"But I like that deuced boarding house. I can come and go as I please without having to listen to Father's various complaints about my behavior."

"He's not so bad. and he wouldn't be so angry with you all the time if you behaved with a little more discretion. How do you expect him to react when you taunt him the way you did last night? That blasted party means a great deal to him."

For once, Dylan decided against a flippant reply. He met Michael's chiding glance head-on, as he tried to find an answer to the question that had haunted him all his life. "You know how hard I've tried to win his favor. I was awarded the bloody VC, for God's sake, and he didn't even come to the ceremony!" His voice rose, and he made an effort to regain control. "He hates me no matter what I do."

Michael looked away. To his credit, he didn't try to deny it.

Watching the play of emotion on his brother's face, Dylan felt a twinge of guilt. He knew Michael didn't enjoy the responsibilities that came with being the heir. And Michael didn't understand any better than Dylan why their father chose to draw a line so sharply between them.

As children, Michael had often tried to take the blame for Dylan's many real and imagined transgressions, wanting to spare his little brother at least some of the constant beatings. But the earl never allowed it.

In their father's eyes, Michael could do no wrong, and Dylan could do no right. "Ah, hell. Let's just change the subject, shall we?" The last thing Dylan wanted to do was dredge up the hurt and pain of the past.

Seeming relieved, Michael cleared his throat and picked at his breakfast. "The old man's been after me to marry. I've begun courting the Duke of Clayton's daughter."

"Lady Natalia?" Dylan pushed away his plate, a sinking feeling in his gut. This was one complication he hadn't counted on.

"I danced with her last night, and she gave me permission to call upon her this morning. She's a strange little thing, a bit too foreign-looking for my tastes. Not much for conversation either, but her dowry is enormous."

"I think she's lovely." Dylan schooled his face into a smile and hoped his anger and dismay didn't show. Everything came so easily to Michael. It seemed Lady Natalia was no exception. Michael had been given permission to call, while Dylan hadn't even been able to win a dance.

Michael raised a brow. "I thought redheaded actresses were more your type."

"So, you've heard about Cassandra." Dylan continued to smile, but he knew what Michael thought. Like Jonathan, Michael assumed no respectable woman would ever look twice at a penniless younger son.

They were probably right.

"I believe everyone has heard about Cassandra." For once, a hint of admiration laced Michael's voice. He leaned forward, rampant curiosity in his warm blue eyes. "What's she like?"

Dylan shrugged. "Beautiful. Sensual. Wildly imaginative."

Michael sighed and leaned back in his chair. "I envy you. It must be nice to have a woman you can relax and be yourself around. Perhaps I'll take a mistress as well, after I'm wed."

A woman you can be yourself around. What a fascinating concept. Dylan decided not to inform his brother he'd never found any such thing. The women he met expected him to be the hero they read about in the papers. He'd never had the courage to disappoint them.

"Why wait until after the wedding?" Dylan asked, truly curious. "Why not take a mistress now?"

"I can't afford even the hint of a scandal," Michael explained, an odd note in his voice. "Not if I'm to win the duke's daughter."

Dylan kept his opinions of his brother's hypocrisy to himself. He finished his breakfast, and then bid Michael farewell. As he hurried from the house, he cursed beneath his breath. Of all the girls in London, why did this bet have to center around the one *Michael* wanted?

He wondered if Jonathan knew about Michael's interest in Lady Natalia. Had the fop put Dylan at odds with his brother on purpose?

The wisest thing to do, given this new information, would be to bow out gracefully and let Jonathan win the infernal wager. He'd come up with the money somehow, even if it meant going to his father.

But as soon as the thought occurred, he dismissed it. He'd never been one to simply give up, and he'd be damned if he'd start now.

Besides, the girl intrigued him, and he was tired of stepping aside for his brother. Perhaps he needed to prove to himself that he could be first in *someone's* heart.

IF YOU'D LIKE TO READ MORE, YOU CAN FIND THE FULL VERSION OF THIS BOOK FOR FREE ON MOST EBOOK RETAILERS, INCLUING AMAZON, BARNES & NOBLE, APPLE iBOOKS, GOOGLE PLAY, AND KOBO.

You can contact Diana at Diana@dianabold.com

Visit her website at www.dianabold.com[1] and sign up for her newsletter!

Like her on Facebook for news and freebies https://www.facebook.com/Dianaboldbooks/

Join Diana's FB Reader Group - https://www.facebook.com/groups/dianasboldbeauties

Diana is also one of the Brazen Belles, a group of twelve similar writers who have a really fun joint FB page! https://www.facebook.com/groups/brazenbelles

OTHER BOOKS BY DIANA BOLD

VICTORIAN ROMANCE

BRIDES OF SCANDAL SERIES

Gambling on the Duke's Daughter

Marrying the American Heiress

Seducing the Spinster

Finding the Black Orchid

UNMASKING PROMETHEUS SERIES

Masked Intentions

Masked Promises

Masked Desires

Dark Intentions

Dark Promises

Dark Desires – Coming soon!

Once a Pirate

---

1.   http://www.dianabold.com

Fortune's Gamble

Queen of May Day

FANTASY ROMANCE

A Knight in Atlantis

The Man from Atlantis – Coming soon!

WESTERN ROMANCE

LAST CHANCE BRIDES SERIES

One Last Chance

Chance of a Lifetime

Love at Last

The Last Bride

Once a Gunslinger

Once a Mail Order Bride

Once a Bandit

Once an Outlaw

Diana Bold has been writing since elementary school and never wanted to be anything but a writer. It took longer than she hoped to accomplish that, but she is now the award-winning author of more than thirty historical romances. She lives in the mountains of Southern Colorado with the love of her life, whom she met rather late in life but was worth the wait. When she's not writing, she enjoys traveling and genealogy.